The Society of Distinguished Lemmings

To Simon – J.C.

A TEMPLAR BOOK

First published in the UK in 2018 by Templar Publishing,
an imprint of Kings Road Publishing, part of the Bonnier Publishing Group,
The Plaza, 535 King's Road, London, SW10 0SZ
www.bonnierpublishing.com

1 3 5 7 9 10 8 6 4 2

ISBN 978-1-78741-054-1

Designed by Olivia Cook
Edited by Ruth Symons

Printed in China

The Society of Distinguished Lemmings

SOCIETY RULES

I.	LEMMINGS ONLY
II.	ALWAYS ACT IN A DISTINGUISHED MANNER
III.	NO UNSEEMLY OR 'WILD' BEHAVIOUR
IV.	NO WALKING ON FOUR LEGS
V.	NO SQUEAKING OR GROWLING
VI.	NO EATING WITH YOUR HANDS
VII.	NO ROLLING
VIII.	NO CLIMBING
IX.	NO MUD
X.	NO QUESTIONING THE RULES

templar
books

Julie Colombet

This is the Society of Distinguished Lemmings.

Deep in their underground burrow, the lemmings follow
a strict set of rules and have a very busy social calendar.

They perform long
and serious plays.

They play the piano exceedingly well!

That said, the Society of Distinguished Lemmings
is not to everyone's taste.

This is Bertie, and he's had enough.
There is TOO MUCH noise in here.

So Bertie has decided to go outside.

Outside, he finds there is a bear.

Bertie has never met a bear before.
He's heard they can be very fierce and scary
(not to mention awfully dim).

And the bear has never met a lemming before.
He's heard they can be talkative and annoying
(not to mention terrible show-offs).

Neither of them moves a muscle.

Then the bear leans down
and gives Bertie
a long, wet
lick.

The bear is clearly in
the mood to make friends!

Bertie shows the bear all his favourite things to do.
But the bear isn't interested in painting . . .

. . . he isn't interested in chess, either. In fact, the bear
isn't interested in anything Bertie suggests.

Apparently the bear would
rather roll in the flowers . . .

. . . or climb a tree . . .

. . . or jump in muddy puddles.

And, much to his surprise, Bertie
finds he'd rather do those things too.

It's not how things are done in the Society (in fact it breaks several rules),
but it's nice to have a friend who's a little bit different.

Bertie and the bear are doing nothing in particular,
when there is a sudden rumbling under the ground . . .

They decide at once that the bear
is not at all distinguished.

If the bear is ever going to join the Society,
he will have a lot to learn.

First of all, he must learn to talk.

ME LEMMING. YOU BEAR.

You can do it!

No roaring, please.

Proper posture is also very important.

Whoa!

This bear has four left feet.

You're doing great!

He trod on my hat!

This doesn't seem very safe if you ask me.

And table manners are a must if he is
ever going to dine in fine society.

But the bear can't do anything right . . .

Before long, the lemmings decide enough is enough.
The bear will never be distinguished. And besides, the lemmings
have better things to do with their time.

It never occurs to them that the bear could be upset. But he is. Because even though he is big and wild and not at all like a lemming, he doesn't want to disappoint Bertie.

But the lemmings have already moved on to other things.

With a lot of talk (but very little thought)
they decide to go on holiday – immediately!

Bertie and the bear haven't been invited, but they don't especially mind.
On their own they can do whatever they like.

They walk to the top of the hill, then Bertie pulls out his book and starts to read aloud.

In the beginning, there was a lemming . . .

And that's when they make a terrible discovery.

"SOMETIMES LEMMINGS WILL DECIDE TO GO ON A VERY LONG JOURNEY
CALLED A MIGRATION. IF THE LEMMINGS TRY TO SWIM TOO FAR,
THEY WILL QUICKLY GROW TIRED AND MAY EVEN DROWN!"

I have a bad feeling about this.

A SHORT HISTORY OF LEMMINGS

Bertie and the bear start to worry.
The lemmings could be in all sorts of trouble without them.

They race across fields . . .

. . . and bound over bushes . . .

. . . and weave through trees . . .

. . . but when they reach the shore, the lemmings have already left.

By now the lemmings are far out to sea. At first they enjoy their swim.

Then they start to grow tired.

And before long, they are exhausted.

The water is deep, the lemmings are tired,
and it is a very long way back to shore . . .

Slowly, a strange shape appears over the horizon.
It grows bigger and bigger, and begins to look oddly familiar.

It's a rescue mission! And it's arrived just in the nick of time.
The lemmings clamber aboard the bear and their
brush with danger is quickly forgotten.

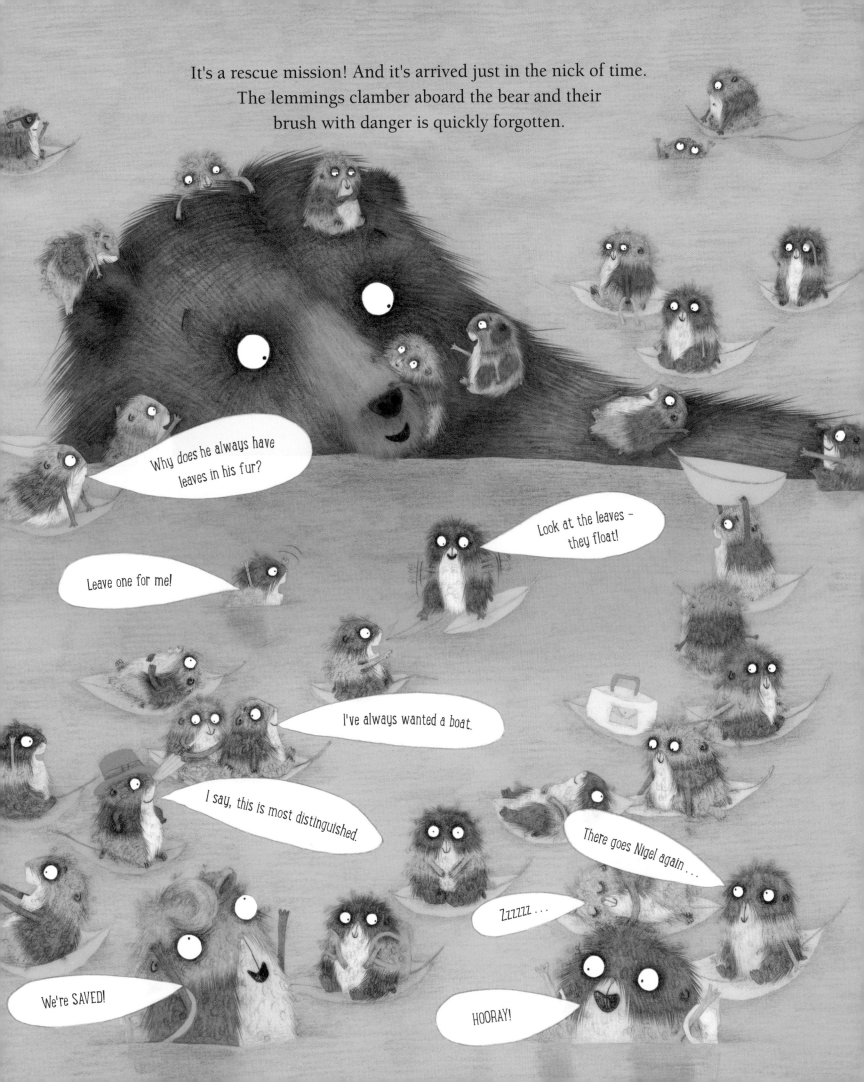

Back on the shore, Bertie calls the Society together for a hasty meeting.
Everyone agrees that the bear must join the Society of Lemmings at once!

With much ceremony (and many long speeches),
the lemmings formally welcome the bear to join them.

More picture books from Templar:

ISBN: 978-1-78370-833-8

ISBN: 978-1-78370-801-7

ISBN: 978-1-78741-008-4 (hardback)
978-1-78370-140-7 (paperback)

ISBN: 978-1-78370-001-1 (hardback)
978-1-78370-062-2 (paperback)